Written by Caron Levis Illustrated by LeUyen Pham

STOP THAT YAWN!

athenum

Atheneum Books for Young Readers
New York London Toronto Sydney New Delhi

abby Wild had had *enough*
of bedtime.
Yawn, curl, snuggle, snore—
What a bore!
She begged Granny to take her away
from Sleepytown.

So they packed their toothbrushes—but no pajamas—and
instead of tucking in . . .

until they reached a place where beds are for bouncing, hushes are shushed, and it's never too late for ice cream.

When the sun went down, Gabby Wild was up, up . . .

So cozy. *So* quiet. *Soooooo* peaceful.

Granny's mouth opened wide.

It grew wide, wide, wider—

Granny, no, we practiced!

Grit your teeth, seal your lips! Whatever you do, don't—

It was too late.
The yawn was on the loose.

Tweeting her whistle and swishing
her click-clacky hair,

Gabby Wild dashed
through the streets,

TOOT BLARE POM·POM·POM

Gabby ran to the Midnight Marching Band for help.

She stomped, snapped, clapped, and tried to warn everyone in sight.

Grit your teeth, seal your lips, we have to stop that—

Gabby tried to get the All-Night Opera to belt.

Using her tickliest feathers, wettest water, and funniest jokes, she fought to keep the audience awake.

With the brightest spotlight
she could shine, Gabby searched
for someone, *anyone*, to stay up with.

But the dogs wouldn't yowl,
the parrots wouldn't squawk.

The picklers wouldn't pickle,
the ice-cream scoopers wouldn't scoop,
the Midnight Marching Band
wouldn't pom-pom-pom;
even the kids wouldn't kick up a fuss.

Nope, all anyone in
Never Sleeping City could do was . . .

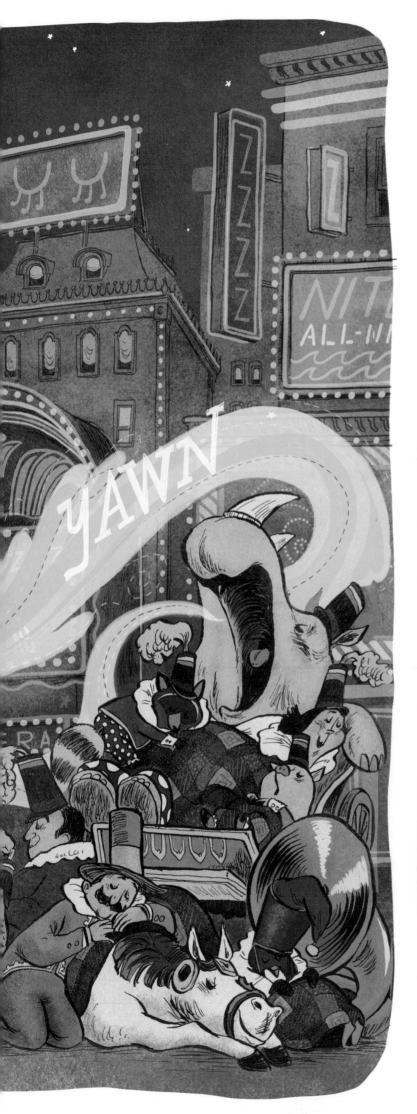

Gabby Wild was horrified. All around her, the city was getting cozy and quiet and peaceful.

There was only one place left for her to turn.

With Never Sleeping City curling and cuddling and snoring all around her, there was only one thing Gabby Wild could do.

She snuggled into Granny's arms.
She got cozy and quiet and peaceful.

Then . . .

she partied all night long in the land
of her wildest dreams.

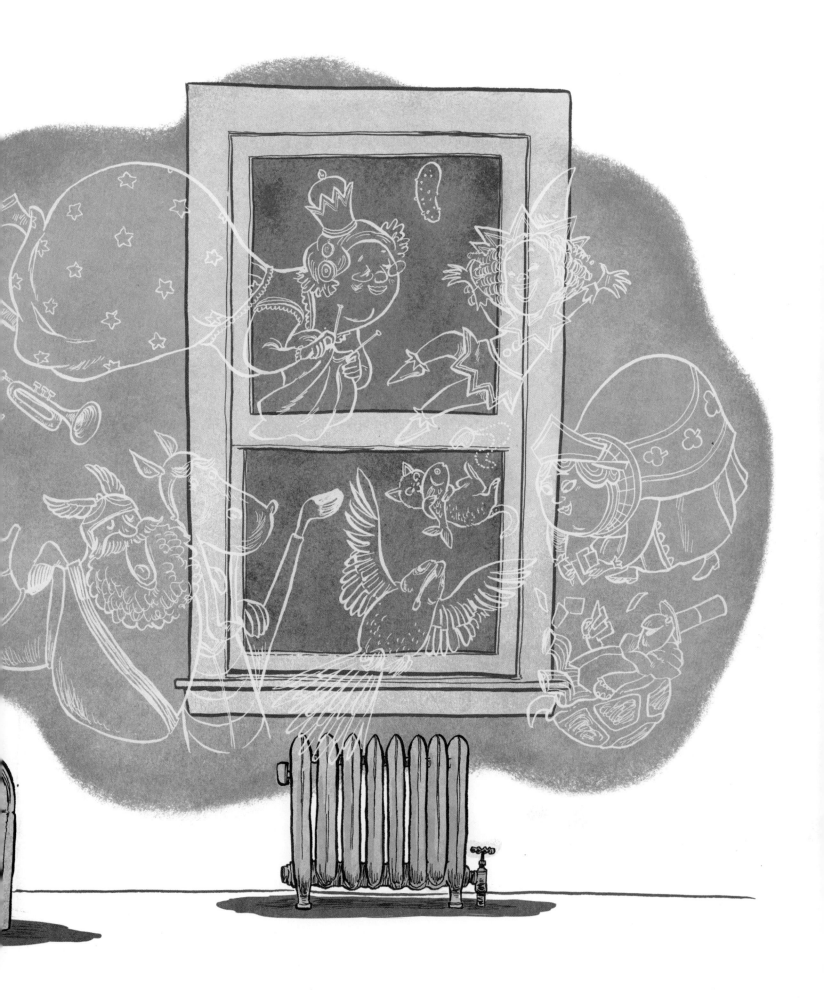

For the wonderful waker-uppers
Ella and Mason, and their grandma,
who unleashes yawns, yet loves tirelessly

And a special coffeepot of thanks
to editor Emma and agent Emily
for Never Sleeping on the job.
—C. L.

To the Frenchmen in my life:
Leo, Adrien, and Alexandre
—L. P.

A
atheneum

ATHENEUM BOOKS FOR YOUNG READERS
An imprint of Simon & Schuster Children's Publishing Division
1230 Avenue of the Americas, New York, New York 10020
Text copyright © 2018 by Caron Levis
Illustrations copyright © 2018 by LeUyen Pham
All rights reserved, including the right of reproduction in whole or in part in any form.
ATHENEUM BOOKS FOR YOUNG READERS is a registered trademark of Simon & Schuster, Inc.
Atheneum logo is a trademark of Simon & Schuster, Inc.
For information about special discounts for bulk purchases, please contact Simon & Schuster Special
Sales at 1-866-506-1949 or business@simonandschuster.com.
The Simon & Schuster Speakers Bureau can bring authors to your live event.
For more information or to book an event, contact the Simon & Schuster Speakers Bureau
at 1-866-248-3049 or visit our website at www.simonspeakers.com.
Jacket design by LeUyen Pham and Semadar Megged; interior design by LeUyen Pham and Lauren Rille
The text for this book was set in Minya Nouvelle.
The illustrations for this book were rendered in croquille and india ink
on bristol board, and colored digitally.
Manufactured in China
0718 SCP
First Edition
2 4 6 8 10 9 7 5 3 1
Library of Congress Cataloging-in-Publication Data
Names: Levis, Caron, author | Pham, LeUyen, illustrator.
Title: Stop that yawn! / written by Caron Levis ; illustrated by LeUyen Pham.
Description: First edition. | New York : Atheneum, [2018] | Summary: Gabby convinces Granny to leave
Sleepytown and stay up all night in a new place, but before long, a contagious yawn takes control.
Identifiers: LCCN 2016030007| ISBN 9781481441797 (hardcover) | ISBN 9781481441803 (eBook)
Subjects: | CYAC: Yawning–Fiction. | Bedtime–Fiction. | Grandmothers–Fiction.
Classification: LCC PZ7.C579695 Sto 2018 | DDC [E]–dc23
LC record available at https://lccn.loc.gov/2016030007